Ollie's New Tricks

by True Kelley

SCHOLASTIC INC.

New York   Toronto   London   Auckland   Sydney
Mexico City   New Delhi   Hong Kong   Buenos Aires

to Sally and Miles Harris

ISBN-13: 978-0-545-08526-7
ISBN-10: 0-545-08526-8

12 11 10 9 8 7 6 5 4 3 2 1   8 9 10 11 12 13/0

Printed in the U.S.A.
First printing, October 2008

Book design by Jennifer Rinaldi Windau

Sam's dog, Ollie, was an old dog.
He was even older than Sam.

Ollie knew a few tricks:

"Sit!"

"Come!"

"Lie down!"

That was it.

Sam wanted Ollie to learn
a new trick.
Ollie was not very interested.

Sam took Ollie's paw.

He pumped it up and down.
"Shake!" he said.

That isn't shaking, thought Ollie.
This *is shaking!*

Sam tried to teach him another trick.
"Beg!" said Sam.

Ollie looked away.
He had his pride.

Sam always left the TV on
while he was at school.
He didn't want Ollie to be bored.

Ollie watched a yoga show.
He learned to do a frog stand.

Then he watched a cooking show.
Ollie made oatmeal cookies.
He ate every single one.

Ollie watched ballroom dancing.
That wasn't so hard.

Sam came home.

Ollie was asleep.

He was very tired from his busy day.

"Sleep!" said Sam.

Ollie woke up.

"Stay!" said Sam.
Ollie got up slowly.
He went over
to his bowl.
Sam thought of
another new trick.

Sam helped Ollie stand up
on his back legs.
"Dance!" said Sam.
Ollie could not believe it.
That was not dancing!
Ollie sat down.
He had his pride.

The next day, Sam left for school.
Ollie watched a skating show.

He went to the closet and found
some skates.
Ollie trotted out to the ice pond.

After a few hours, he could do
a "Backward Flying Swan!"

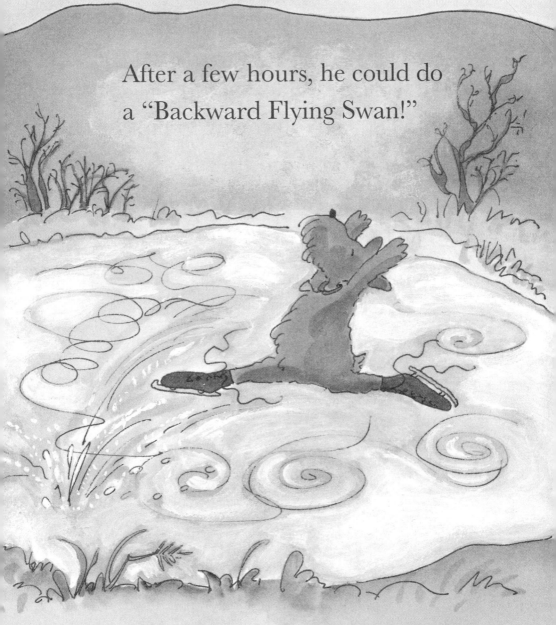

Then he went home.
He put the skates away and
went to sleep.

Sam came home.

He woke up Ollie.

Sam showed Ollie how to flip
a treat into his mouth.

It was embarrassing to watch.

Ollie looked away.

He had his pride.

The next day, Ollie learned
how to read.
He was a very fast reader, too!

He read a book about origami.

Next he read a book
about computers.
Soon he was typing away.

Ollie found out how to knit socks.

He read about building a rocket.
Scuba diving looked interesting, too.

Ollie learned some magic tricks.

That was a busy day!
Learning to drive a car would have
to wait until tomorrow.

Sam came home.
Ollie was asleep on the couch.
Sam found a sock on the floor.
He tossed it to the other side of
the living room.
"Fetch!" he said.

Ollie got up.

He stretched and yawned.

He went over to his bowl.

"You are too old to learn new tricks,"
sighed Sam.

He scratched Ollie behind the ears.

"But you are a very good old dog."

Sam came home the next day.
Something was wrong.

The TV was turned off.
Ollie was lying in the middle
of the floor with his feet in the air.

"Oh no! Poor old Ollie!" Sam said.

Sam started to cry.

Ollie opened one eye.

Then Ollie sat up!

"Ollie!" said Sam. "You were only
playing!"
Sam hugged Ollie.
"You learned a new trick!" said Sam.

Ollie went over to his bowl.
He had his pride.

Tomorrow he might show Sam
a few simple dance steps.